This book belongs to:

. . . .

. . . .

Retold by Monica Hughes
Illustrated by Gwyneth Williamson

Reading consultants: Betty Root and Monica Hughes

Marks and Spencer p.l.c.
PO Box 3339
Chester, CH99 9QS

shop online
www.marksandspencer.com

ISBN 978-1-84805-330-4
Printed in China

Beauty
and the
Beast

MARKS &
SPENCER

Helping your child to read

First Readers are closely linked to the National Curriculum. Their vocabulary has been carefully selected from the word lists recommended by the National Literacy Strategy.

Read the story
Read the story
to your child
a few times.

Suddenly there was a terrible roar.
An ugly beast appeared.
"Why have you stolen my rose?" said the Beast.
"The red rose is for my daughter," said the father.
"Take the rose," said the Beast. "But you must give me your daughter in return, or you will die."

16

Follow your finger
Run your finger under
the text as you read.
Your child will soon begin to
follow the words with you.

Look at the pictures
Talk about the pictures. They will help your child to understand the story.

"Why have you stolen my rose?" said the Beast.

17

Have a go
Let your child have a go at reading the large type on each right-hand page. It repeats a line from the story.

Join in
When your child is ready, encourage them to join in with the main story text. Shared reading is the first step to reading alone.

Once upon a time there was a girl
called Beauty.
She lived with her father and two
greedy sisters.
Beauty was kind and good.

Beauty was kind and good.

One day her father was going to town. "I will bring you each a present," he said.

"I want a new dress," said the first sister.

"I want a new hat," said the second sister.

"I would like a red rose," said Beauty.

"I would like a red rose,"
said Beauty.

The father went to town but he could not find a red rose.
On the way back it began to snow.
He could not see the way.
Soon the father was lost.
As if by magic, a castle appeared.

Soon the father was lost.

The father went inside.
There was no one inside.
But it was warm and cosy.
And there was food to eat.

In the morning the father set off home
again.
There was a rose bush in the castle
garden.
The father thought of Beauty's present.
So he picked one red rose.

He picked one red rose.

Suddenly there was a terrible roar.
An ugly beast appeared.
"Why have you stolen my rose?" said
the Beast.
"The red rose is for my daughter," said
the father.
"Take the rose," said the Beast. "But
you must give me your daughter in
return, or you will die."

"Why have you stolen my
rose?" said the Beast.

The father went home.
He told his daughters about the
ugly Beast.
"I will go to the Beast," said Beauty.

"I will go to the Beast,"
said Beauty.

When Beauty got to the castle she
went inside.
There was no one inside.
But it was warm and cosy.
And there was food to eat.

Every evening the ugly Beast appeared.
He was good and kind to Beauty.
Beauty grew to like the Beast.

Beauty grew to like the Beast.

One evening the Beast gave Beauty a
magic mirror.
Beauty looked in the mirror.
She saw her father was ill.
"I must go to my father," said Beauty.
"Promise me you will come back after
three nights," said the Beast.

Beauty went home.
She looked after her father.
After three nights he was better.
But she forgot her promise to the Beast.

Beauty went home.

One day Beauty looked in the magic
mirror.
She saw that the Beast was ill.
Then she remembered her promise.
"I must go back to the Beast," said
Beauty.

She went back to the castle.
The Beast lay beside the red rose bush.
"Please do not die, Beast," said Beauty.
"I love you."

"I must go back to the Beast."

As if by magic, the Beast changed into a handsome prince.

"I was under a magic spell," said the prince. "But your kind words broke the spell."

Soon after, Beauty and the prince were married and they lived happily ever after.

The Beast changed into
a handsome prince.

Look back in your book.
Can you read these words?

Beauty

Beast

rose

father

sisters

Can you answer these questions?

What present did
Beauty want?

Who went to live
with the Beast?

What
happened to
the Beast?

Read Together

Look out for other books in the **First Readers** range (subject to availability):

Fairytale Readers

Hansel and Gretel | Goldilocks and the Three Bears | Jack and the Beanstalk | Beauty and the Beast

The Enormous Turnip | The Elves and the Shoemaker | The Emperor's New Clothes | Cinderella

The Three Billy Goats Gruff | The Three Little Pigs | The Princess and the Pea